NO LONGER PROPERTY OF
SEATTLE PUBLIC LIBRARY

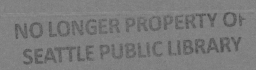

For Dad
love,
Eldest Dort
x

BAiLEY & BLANKET

BY EMiLY HOUSE

BLUE DOT KIDS PRESS

Bailey and Blanket were the best of friends
from the moment they first found each other.

Bailey was tiny, in need of some warmth,
and Blanket was a soft, cozy cover.

Everywhere Bailey went,
Blanket went too. They loved
to adventure together

to the shops with Dad
or to the park with Mom,
side by side whatever the weather.

Blanket was the perfect
parachute for a daredevil
flying high in the sky.

Blanket was the cleverest
hiding place when the scary
monsters crept by.

Blanket was the finest
sail to help conquer
all seven seas.

Blanket was the comfiest
hammock for relaxing with
a good book to read.

Blanket was
a magical tent
on a rainy and
dull afternoon.

Blanket was the greatest
companion for gazing
at the stars and the moon.

Brave Blanket even survived the trials
of Dad's spring cleaning routine,

spinning around . . . and around . . . and around . . . and around . . .

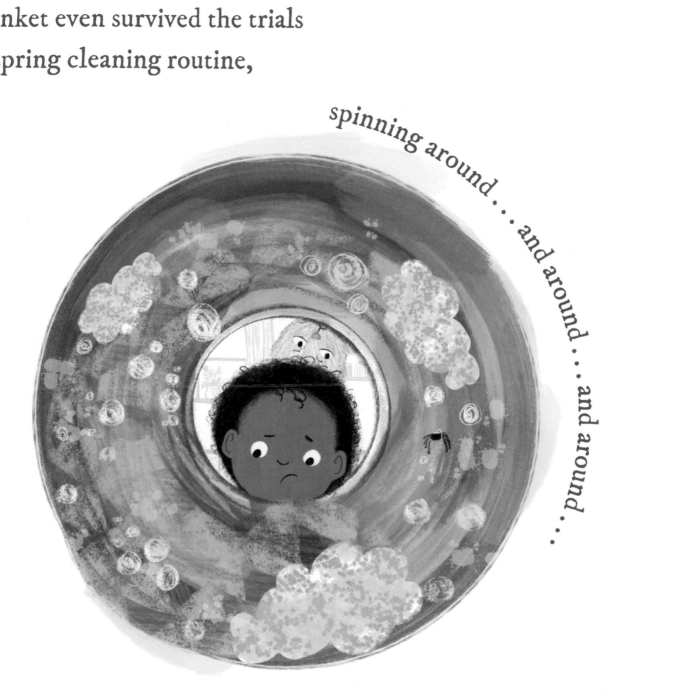

in the suds of
the washing machine!

One day, the family was out on a picnic,
and Bailey was down by the lake.
Suddenly, a dog snatched Blanket
and tried to make its escape.

"Oh no!" cried Mom.
"Rascal pup!" exclaimed Dad.
Bailey ran after the dog.

"Come back here
with my friend!"
Bailey shouted,
as the thief
hurdled a big
wooden log.

Soon Bailey caught up
and, with no thought of peril,
began to battle the hound . . .

Bailey tried and tried, but the
great tug-of-war soon saw Blanket
in shreds on the ground.

That night Bailey lay, face in the pillow,
crying, lonely, and sad.
Life would lack adventure without Blanket . . .
I'll make a plan, thought Dad.

So, while Bailey slept, Dad gathered dear Blanket
and all of the tattered threads.
He grabbed his flashlight, made a mug of hot tea,
and marched to his garden shed.

I know it's here somewhere,
he mumbled.
I wish I were more organized!

He rummaged and managed
to find what was needed
to make Bailey a special surprise.

SEWING KIT

Bailey woke the next morning, still gloomy,
and sleepily got out of bed,
just in time to see Dad run triumphantly
up the path from his garden shed.

"Surprise!" cheered Dad, giving Bailey
a parcel clutched tight in his hands,
carefully wrapped in newspaper,
held together by three rubber bands.

"Blanket was broken, too broken to fix,
and I knew how that made you so sad,
but I've worked through the night with my needle,
and now Blanket's torn scraps . . .

are a BAG!

As you grow, if you ever feel lonely,
you can be sure that Blanket's still there.
Not as a warm, cozy cover
but as this pack you can wear."

"Oh, Blanket." Bailey smiled. "I love the new you.
Thanks, Dad, you are so very clever."
Reunited, the two friends set off to enjoy
more happy adventures together.

Blue Dot Kids Press

www.BlueDotKidsPress.com

Original North American edition published in 2022 by Blue Dot Kids Press, PO Box 2344, San Francisco, CA 94126. Blue Dot Kids Press is a trademark of Blue Dot Publications LLC.

Original North American edition © 2022 Blue Dot Publications LLC

© Text and Illustrations: Emily House, 2021

First published in South Africa in 2021 by Imagnary House as *Bonbon and Blanket* © Imagnary House, 2021. English translation rights arranged through S.B.Rights Agency, Stephanie Barrouillet. This North American edition is published under exclusive license with Imagnary House.

Original North American edition edited by Summer Dawn Laurie and designed by Teresa Bonaddio

All rights reserved under all applicable laws. No part of this publication may be reproduced, distributed, or transmitted in any form by any means, including photocopying, recording, or other mechanical or electronic methods, without the prior written permission from Blue Dot Kids Press. To request permissions or to order copies of this publication, contact the publisher at www.BlueDotKidsPress.com.

BLUE DOT KIDS PRESS

Cataloging in Publication Data is available from the United States Library of Congress.

ISBN: 9781737603221

The illustrations in the book are digitally created through Procreate on the iPad.

Printed in China with soy inks.

First Printing